When Witches' Wands Won't Work

Illustrated by Poly Bernatene

For Paula, with love. P.B.

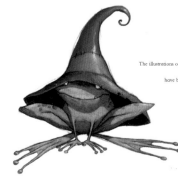

First published in 2005
by Meadowside Children's Books
185 Fleet Street, London EC4A 2HS

Text © Meadowside Children's Books 2004
Illustrations © Poly Bernatene 2004
The illustrations originally appeared in part in "Las brujas Paca y Poca y su gato Espantoso" by Cristina Portorrico.
The rights of Poly Bernatene to be identified as the illustrator of this work
have been asserted by him in accordance with the Copyright, Designs and Patents Act, 1988

A CIP catalogue record for this book is available from the British Library
Printed in U.A.E.

10 9 8 7 6 5 4 3 2 1

meadowside
CHILDREN'S BOOKS

This is a story about
a witch called Rattle,
a witch called Ricket
and their cat (called Rum).

This is Ricket.
(she is clever
at spooking
spiders)

One evening, after a hard day's potion-mixing, the two witches settled down to the usual evening activities with a deep sigh.

"I'm fed up,"
groaned Rattle.
"Me too,"
moaned Ricket.
"Let's go on holiday!"

Rattle packed the wands, the hats and the swimsuits.
(She's very organised)

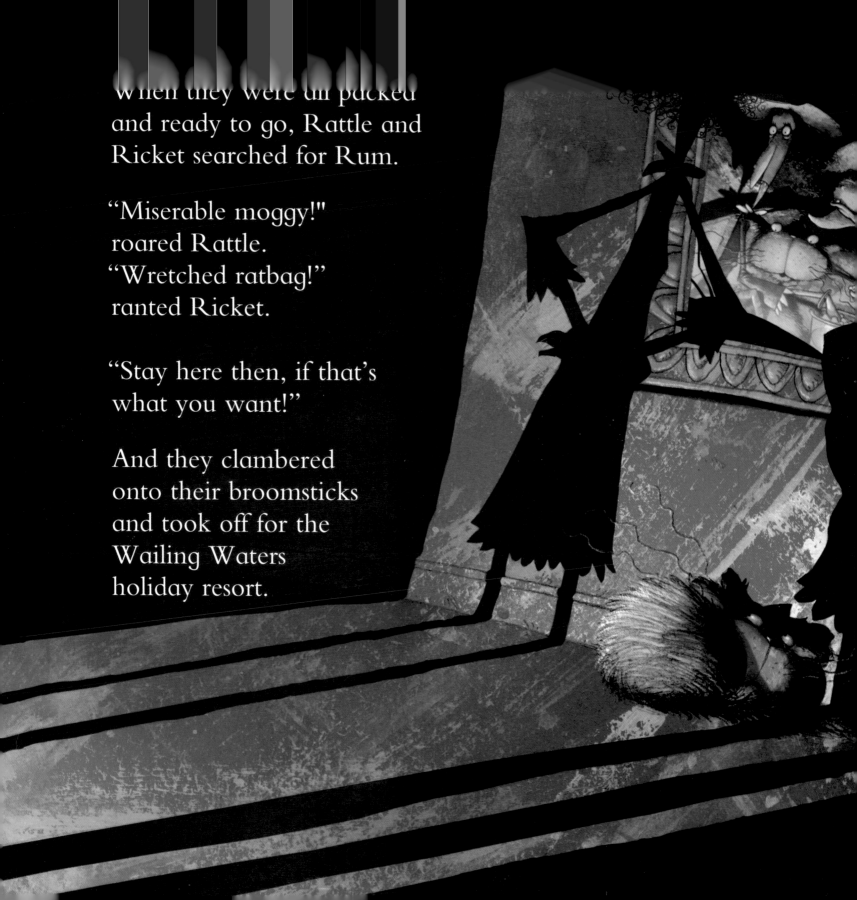

When they were all packed and ready to go, Rattle and Ricket searched for Rum.

"Miserable moggy!" roared Rattle. "Wretched ratbag!" ranted Ricket.

"Stay here then, if that's what you want!"

And they clambered onto their broomsticks and took off for the Wailing Waters holiday resort.

With Rattle and Ricket gone,
Rum was free to roam.

He stared out of the window
wondering how to make
the most of his freedom.

And just then he saw a
circus passing by.

"I've always wanted to be in a circus," thought Rum.
(He was an excellent tightrope walker)

"The horrible hags will never miss me."
(And he was off!)

Back at the wailing waters, the wallowing
witches were having a whale of a time
with their fiendish friends.

All was peaceful and everyone
was relaxed.

The wind
whipped
through
the waving
branches.

Rattle had
a paddle.

Ricket did
some fishing.

The little monsters
were happy
feeding Daddy
some bats.

(Mummy ran away)

As Rattle and Ricket
languished at the lagoon,
Rum had run away.

At the circus, the red-faced ringleader
watched the acrobatic cat as he
teetered on a tightrope.

"Aha," he said to himself with
a sinister smile.
"This moggy means money."

And the wretched
ringleader locked
the performing
pet in a cage.
(He wasn't a
nice man)

The next day, as Ricket was
unpacking at the haunted holiday
house, Rattle rushed into the room.

"Look at this!" she shrieked, holding
up a poster she had found outside.
"That circus star looks like Rum."
"It is Rum!" replied Ricket.
"It can't be Rum!" retorted Rattle.
"It is Rum!" roared her sister.
"Rum's run away to the circus.
We have to get him back!"

Rattle and Ricket rummaged in their
luggage for their wands.

Bother! Both were broken!

(Well, Ricket is horribly heavy)

Waving their wobbly wands, Rattle and Ricket jumped onto their broomsticks and raced towards the big top. They scoured and searched everywhere before finally they found the cage that contained their captured cat.

Zzzap!

They waved their wands… but nothing happened.

"What will we do?" wailed the worried witches.

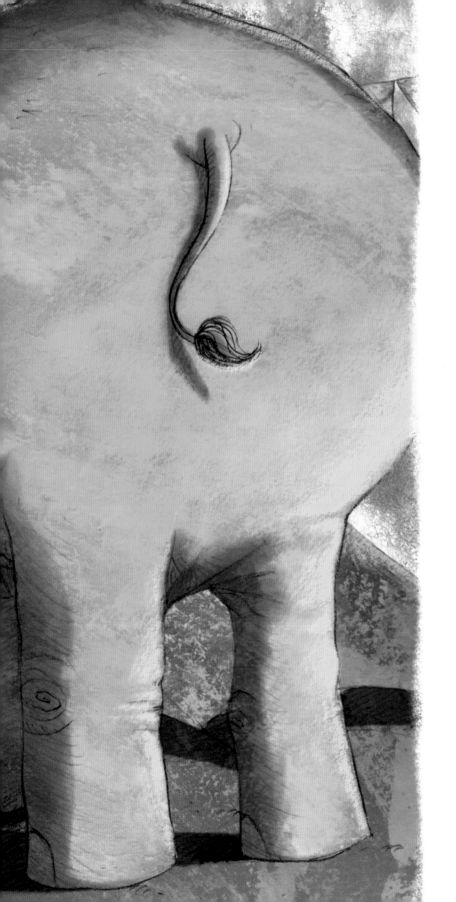

Rickett ran and grabbed a passing elephant and carried him back to the cage.

"Trumpet, snort, trumpet, honk" said Rattle. (who could speak fluent Elephant)

"Meeeoow!" said Rum. (who couldn't)

The elephant (who was happy to help) used all his strength to bend the bars and Rum was free!

But as he leapt from his cage Rum spotted the red-faced ringleader, rushing towards him in a rage.

Rum sunk his claws into the ringleader's head.

MEOWW!

"Our wands aren't working!" said Ricket. "What do we do now?!"

Just as the rascal rushed past, the elephant stepped forward and trod on the ringleader's toe.

Squelch!

The ringleader
wailed and
wept, then
sobbed and
snivelled, then
promised to be
good from now on.

Sniff...

Rattle's
broomstick gave
the ringleader a
whacking wallop.

Thwak!

From that day on (and just to prove how nice he could be), every day was a party!

Which means that, once again, we're back where we started with Rattle (who is now making her fortune in the circus),

Ricket (who looks after the fortune teller's baby),